MW00877769

For pickleball players

I LIKE TO READ is a registered trademark of Holiday House Publishing, Inc.

Text and illustrations copyright © 2024 by Paul Meisel
All Rights Reserved
HOLIDAY HOUSE is registered in the U.S. Patent and Trademark Office.
Printed and bound in January 2024 at C&C Offset, Shenzhen, China.
The artwork was created with watercolor, acrylic, and pencil
on Saunders Waterford paper with digital enhancements.
www.holidayhouse.com
First Edition
1 3 5 7 9 10 8 6 4 2

Library of Congress Cataloging-in-Publication Data is available.

ISBN: 978-0-8234-5560-7 (hardcover)

I Like to Read® books, created by award-winning picture book artists as well as talented newcomers, instill confidence and the joy of reading in new readers.

We want to hear every new reader say, "I like to read!"

Visit our website for flashcards, activities and more about the series:
www.holidayhouse.com/I-Like-to-Read/
#ILTR
This book has been officially leveled by using the
F&P Text Level Gradient™ Leveling System.

I See a Rat

PAUL MEISEL

I Like to Read®

HOLIDAY HOUSE • NEW YORK

What is that?

It is fast.

It is gone.

"Hello, Dog!" says Rat.

"You are my new friend, Rat," says Dog.